SOCK MONKEY
TAKES A BATH

Cece Bell

CANDLEWICK PRESS

For Tom, and in memory of
Henry

First edition in this format 2015

Library of Congress Cataloging-in-Publication Data is available.
Library of Congress Catalog Card Number 2003040982

ISBN 978-0-7636-1962-6 (original hardcover)
ISBN 978-0-7636-7759-6 (reformatted hardcover)

15 16 17 18 19 20 CCP 10 9 8 7 6 5 4 3 2 1

Printed in Shenzhen, Guangdong, China

This book was typeset in Cafeteria.
The illustrations were created digitally.

Candlewick Press
99 Dover Street
Somerville, Massachusetts 02144

visit us at www.candlewick.com

One day, Sock Monkey, the famous actor,
received a special delivery.

It was an invitation to attend the Oswald Awards! He was a nominee for Best Supporting Toy in a motion picture!

YiPPee!

Sock Monkey hopped with excitement.

But as he read on, the last words on the invitation made him gasp.

As a NOMINEE* for BEST SUPPORTING TOY in a MOTION PICTURE, you are cordially invited to the OSWALD AWARDS at the BIG THEATER.

*Nominees MUST be Clean.

R.S.V.P.

CLEAN? He had to be clean?

Once, long ago, Sock Monkey had been a spotless monkey. His whites were like the purest snow, his reds like the ripest apples, and his browns like a freshly pressed suit.

But Sock Monkey had been very active over the years . . .

and he had never, not once in his life, ever taken a bath.
Never. Now he was downright filthy.

Just thinking about taking a bath made Sock Monkey dizzy with fear.

A bath? Oh no!

The stinky soap! The icy water! The scratchy towels!

A BATH WILL MAKE ME NOTHING MORE THAN a BLOTCHY, LUMPY, SHRUNKEN MONKEY!

But what if Sock Monkey won the Oswald and he wasn't there to accept it?

He had no choice. He *had* to get clean. So Sock Monkey turned to his friends for help.

Will you help me?

Certainly!

Of course!

What are friends for?

"The first step," said Miss Bunn, "is to be gently hand-washed in warm soapy water."

So Miss Bunn flew Sock Monkey to the warm Simian Springs, in the Mystical Monkey Mountains . . .

where a group of wild bathing monkeys carefully
washed him with a very mild soap.

"The next step," said Froggie, "is to rinse out all the soap with clear cool water."

So Froggie rowed Sock Monkey to the middle of the perfectly pure Lilypad Pond . . .

and Sock Monkey rinsed out all the soap by
swimming a few laps in the clear cool water.

"The final step," said Blue Pig, "is to lie on a soft fluffy towel for a good long while, until you are dry."

So Blue Pig drove Sock Monkey to the hot Sahara Sands . . .

Mmm. Sweet warmth.

and Sock Monkey basked all day in the sizzling sunshine.

At last, Sock Monkey was washed and dry. His friends could hardly wait to see his new look . . .

Now Sock Monkey could attend the awards show . . . and maybe win an Oswald!

Sock Monkey rented a tuxedo, and his friends helped him get ready for his big night.

Then a limo came and picked him up.

Sock Monkey couldn't believe he was finally there —
the Oswald Awards at the Big Theater!

He glided down the red carpet, while the other toys
greeted him with exclamations of astonishment.

Miss Bunn, Froggie, and Blue Pig watched the show on TV at home.

Sock Monkey looked nervous.

When the big moment finally arrived, Sock Monkey
was ready to burst.

"And the nominees are...

TEDDY BEAR!

SOCK MONKEY!

JACK-IN-THE-BOX!

BABY DOLL!

Who would win the Oswald?

"AND THE OSWALD FOR BEST SUPPORTING TOY IN A MOTION PICTURE GOES TO . . .

JACK-in-the-BOX!

Sock Monkey was disappointed. He watched in envy as
Jack accepted his Oswald.

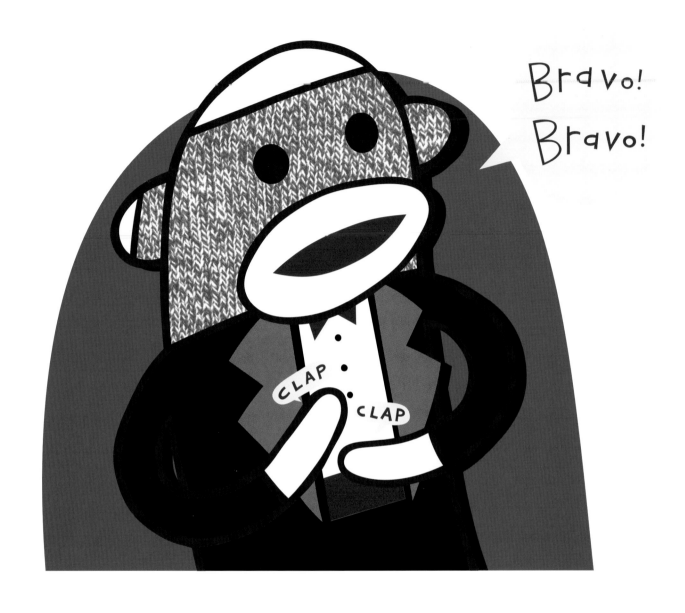

But Sock Monkey was feeling fresh and clean — and Jack really was a talented actor. So Sock Monkey decided right then and there to celebrate Jack's success.

He was chatting with a famous actress and relishing a tasty bit of cheese when he heard another announcement:

THE ICHABOD THALBURG AWARD FOR CLEANEST NOMINEE GOES TO . . .

The crowd went wild.

Sock Monkey bounced up to the stage, feeling prouder and cleaner than he had ever felt in his whole life.

"I'd like to thank the judges," said Sock Monkey as he accepted his very own Oswald.

"And give a special thank-you to my best friends — Miss Bunn, Froggie, and Blue Pig. I couldn't have done it without them."

THE END